JEANNE WILLIS   JENNI DESMOND

RAAAR

BLUE MONSTER WANTS IT ALL!

LITTLE TIGER

LONDON

Blue Monster loved brand new things more than anything.

When he was a baby, he said,
"I don't want my old pram.
I want a new one!"

He wouldn't stop screaming
until he got it.
But . . .

. . . it didn't make him happy for long.
"I don't want my old teddy!" he said.
"I want a new thing to cuddle!"
And he threw it out of the pram.
So . . .

. . . his mum and dad gave him
a baby sister. Blue Monster
loved cuddling her at first.

But he soon got bored.

PARP

"I don't want my old sister!" he yelled.
"I don't want my old teddy!
 Or my old mum and dad!"

He took all the money his
old granny had given him and
left home to start a new life.

Blue Monster bought himself a new hat.

He liked it so much,
he wore it all morning.
But that afternoon
he said ...

… "I don't want this old hat!
I want something new!"
He stamped his hat flat
and bought …

a shiny, red racing car. He was
pleased with it in every way.

BEEP

But the next day, Blue Monster didn't like it one bit. "I don't want my old car!" he screamed. "I want to buy a great, big golden palace with a funfair and a circus!"

Which he did. And it was wonderful. But only
for a while. "What I really need is a new . . ."

... "aeroplane!" said Blue Monster. So he bought a jumbo jet and flew off ...

. . . to a tropical island near New Guinea.
"This looks like paradise!" said Blue Monster.
So he bought the whole island and
everything in it. But . . .

... he didn't want the old animals who lived there. So he bought new gorillas, new polar bears, new zebras and . . .

a new submarine, so he could watch his new whales.

That night, he climbed into his
new hammock.

"I've bought everything I need
to make me happy now," he smiled.
Then he drifted off to sleep beneath
the stars.

Blue Monster woke up to a brand new day.
His new birds were singing. His new bees
were buzzing. The sun was shining
but he still wasn't happy.

"I don't want that old sun!"
he said. "I want a new one!"

And he snatched it out of the sky and
he ATE it! Everything went dark.

Blue Monster was cold and scared and alone.
He really needed a hug but none of his
new things could comfort him.

"Never mind,"
he sniffed. "I'll go and
buy myself a new . . ."

"...family!"

But there are some things money just can't buy.

There were no families for sale.

Or friends.

Blue Monster began to sob. He sobbed
so hard, he spat out the sun.

Suddenly, he saw the light.

"I don't *need* a new family!"
he cried. "I love . . ."

"...my old family!"

Blue Monster fixed his broken plane,
and flew all the way home...

...to give his old mum, his old dad and his old sister a good old hug. This made Blue Monster feel a hundred times happier than new hats, fast planes and paradise islands ever could.

Because...

... he had **everything** he could ever need.